W.R. Wilde

# Medico-Legal Observations upon the Case of Amos Greenwood

Anatiposi

**W.R. Wilde**

# Medico-Legal Observations upon the Case of Amos Greenwood

Reprint of the original.

1st Edition 2023 | ISBN: 978-3-38230-520-8

Anatiposi Verlag is an imprint of Outlook Verlagsgesellschaft mbH.

Verlag (Publisher): Outlook Verlag GmbH, Zeilweg 44, 60439 Frankfurt, Deutschland
Vertretungsberechtigt (Authorized to represent): E. Roepke, Zeilweg 44, 60439 Frankfurt, Deutschland
Druck (Print): Books on Demand GmbH, In de Tarpen 42, 22848 Norderstedt, Deutschland

# MEDICO-LEGAL OBSERVATIONS

UPON THE

# CASE OF AMOS GREENWOOD,

TRIED

## AT THE LIVERPOOL ASSIZES, DECEMBER, 1857,

FOR THE

## WILFUL MURDER OF MARY JOHNSON, AND SENTENCED TO PENAL SERVITUDE FOR LIFE.

BY

## W. R. WILDE, F. R. C. S. I.,

SURGEON TO ST. MARK'S HOSPITAL, DUBLIN.

DUBLIN:

M<sup>c</sup>GLASHAN & GILL, 50 UPPER SACKVILLE-STREET.

1859.

# CASE OF AMOS GREENWOOD.

In the "Times" of Monday, the 7th of December, 1857, I read an
account of the trial of Amos Greenwood, aged 22, for the wilful
murder of Mary Johnson, a child under ten years of age, who
died, as was alleged, from mortification, the result of violence
and disease received during sexual connexion perpetrated on
the 22nd of October previously. I was much struck by the
account given in the newspaper: having, as many of my
readers are aware, paid some attention to the medico-legal
question of rape, and written a little work upon the subject[a],
I felt that this might possibly have been a case in which an
error had been committed, from popular prejudice, on the one
hand, and mistaken medical opinion on the other. I therefore
immediately communicated my suspicions to my friend Mr.
Lawrence of London, who, in reply, stated that he also had
been struck with the peculiarity of the case as reported, agreed
with me as to the likelihood of a mistake having been made,
and advised me to communicate with the Judge who had tried
it, to whom he had also written upon the subject. Out of that
communication has arisen the following statement. Before
however, I proceed to discuss the evidence, I beg to premise a
brief history of the case, every particle of which was sworn to,
as I learned from attested copies of the depositions of the witnesses, and of the statements made both at the coroner's inquest
and the trial.

The parents of the deceased Mary Johnson, as well as all the
other parties connected with this case, were in a very humble
walk of life—costermongers—who "obtained their livelihood
by travelling about the country with a stall, for the purpose of
selling fruit, &c., at the various fairs and markets." In October
the little girl was employed to take care of a baby by a Mr.
and Mrs. Handcock, who were in the same line of business.
About the middle of the month Greenwood was also hired
by the Handcocks to assist in their vocation. On Thursday,
the 22nd of October, this family proceeded to Heap, a village
near Manchester, where a fair was about to be held. That
night the whole family, composed of five individuals, slept in

[a] Medico-Legal Observations upon Infantile Leucorrhœa. London: Churchill.
1853.

a lodging-house, in one small room, in which were two beds, one occupied by the Handcocks and their child, and the other by Amos Greenwood and Mary Johnson. The latter went to bed first, about half-past 7 o'clock; Greenwood followed in about two hours; and within a quarter of an hour or twenty minutes the Handcocks retired to rest. The room was very small, and the beds were within a yard of each other. No disturbance occurred, and no complaint was made during the night. Early the next morning they all took the train for Wigan fair, Mrs. Handcock packing up, and " taking with them the bed on which the prisoner and the deceased slept, as it was the one usually kept and used in the booth or caravan, on their travels from place to place:" she did not notice any stain or other mark upon it. Mary Johnson made no complaint, and appeared to be in perfect health all that day, (Friday), also the next day (Saturday); and up to Sunday evening, when it was remarked that she walked lame, and appeared to be in pain; when questioned, she complained, in the presence of the prisoner and a woman named Butterworth, of a " smarting in her thighs." She was sent to bed early; and upon being examined by her mistress her genitals were found to be sore, and her thighs excoriated. All that night she complained of great pain, and the next morning she was brought to Mr. Winnard, surgeon, of Wigan, who examined her, believed the case to be one of vaginitis, prescribed an astringent lotion and some purgative medicine, informing her friends that she was very ill, and would require much attention. Mr. Winnard saw them twice; no accusation was made in his presence on either occasion; no suspicion raised as to the cause; but the people asked him " if swallowing a sixpence could cause the state the child was in." That evening Mrs. Handcock and the girl proceeded to Heywood, where her disease grew rapidly worse. She was then pressed by her friends to confess to the cause of her ailment, but for a long time she continued to protest in having nothing to confess, although, as shown by the depositions, several suggestions were made to her by the females who surrounded her. Finally she was told that, unless she made a confession, she should be left to die, " as that nothing would do her good." It is asserted that she then stated that upon the night when they all slept in the same room at Heap, and while in the bed adjoining her mistress, her bed-fellow, Amos Greenwood, had connexion with her, and produced the violence which her person then exhibited.

An unlicensed practitioner was then called in, who put her upon the use of mercury. Sloughing and mortification set in, and proceeded with great rapidity; then Mr. Pickford, surgeon of Heywood, saw her; he discontinued the mercury, and prescribed bark. A magistrate took her deposition on the 2nd of November, but not as a "dying deposition," although afterwards used at the trial. The girl's symptoms proceeded with great rapidity, the mortification extending over the pubes in front, and the whole of the nates behind. She died on Thursday, the 5th of November, about thirteen days after the alleged intercourse, and ten from the first discovery of the disease. A post-mortem examination was made, and a coroner's inquest held. The prisoner was arrested, and found to have venereal warts on his penis. Mr. Jameson, who first attended her at Heywood, swore she died of " mortification of the genitals, brought on by laceration, inflammation, and venereal poison."

The case was tried at Liverpool on the 5th of December. The jury found the prisoner guilty of manslaughter, and Mr. Justice Wightman sentenced him to penal servitude for the term of his natural life.

In my letter to the Judge, dated 11th December, I endeavoured to point out what appeared to me unexplained questions suggested by the trial—called his attention to the cases related by Percival and Kinder Wood, showing that medical men were occasionally mistaken; and that, even if it were venereal she had, the child, having slept in the same bed with the prisoner from the 14th to the 22nd of October, might have been infected without any attempt at connexion. I stated that I could not find any record of death from mortification in a child like Mary Johnson, as the result of gonorrhœa or syphilis; and I pointed out how prone to deceive children are in cases of leucorrhœa, &c. Mr. Lawrence's letter was somewhat to the same effect.

His Lordship was good enough to reply on the 19th of the same month, and among other matters said:—" It was proved to the satisfaction of the jury that the prisoner, who slept with the deceased, a female child of nine years of age, had *forcible* connexion with her, and that her private parts had been *dreadfully lacerated*, and the *perineum ruptured;* that the prisoner was at the time labouring under the venereal in a very advanced stage; and that when the medical men saw the child, which was not until several days had elapsed, she exhibited symptoms of the venereal disease, attended with inflammation so violent, that the parts mortified, and she died. The cause of death was not attributed to the disease *only,* but to the disease and the laceration. There may be infantile diseases which in their symptoms so closely resemble syphilis that they may be mistaken for it; but in the present case why should the symptoms be attributed to some infantile complaint rather than to the venereal disease, when it was proved that the man who had connexion with her was infected with that complaint in a high degree?"

Still not feeling satisfied, from the history of the case and the symptoms, that the child died either of syphilis or from forced connexion, or both, I entered into communication with Mr. Cobbett, the lawyer who was assigned by the Judge *at the trial* to defend the prisoner, after he had been arraigned; and through his kindness I procured copies of the depositions, the Crown briefs, and also a history of those portions of the case which did not appear in the newspapers. I also communicated with the several practitioners who examined the deceased; and having satisfied myself that the child died of that description of unhealthy, spontaneous inflammation, analogous to *cancrum oris*, which occasionally attacks persons at her time of life, now known as *Noma Pudendi*,—I drew up the following statement, which I then forwarded, together with the list of questions, given at page 69, to twelve medical men, whose opinions, from their knowledge of the subject, as well as their high standing in the profession, would, I thought, entitle them to consideration:—

" At the recent Liverpool Assizes, Amos Greenwood, aged 23, was indicted for the murder of Mary Johnson, a perfectly healthy child under ten years of age, and was found guilty of manslaughter. The cause of death was stated to be rape and venereal. The prisoner and deceased slept, in the same bed, in a room with the other members of the family with whom they resided. On the night of the 22nd of October, 1857, the persons who slept in the same room swore to there having been no cries or any noise whatever during the night. The girl rose the next morning, and went to her work as usual, made no complaint, and uttered no expression of pain. Three days afterwards, a woman, remarking that she seemed to be in pain, examined her, and found her sore in the genitals. The child is said to have stated that the prisoner had had connexion with her on the night of the 22nd, and had 'hurt her greatly.' She was taken to a medical practitioner on the 26th, who seemed to make light of the matter, and gave her some medicine. On the 27th she got worse, and two other practitioners were called in, who stated that the perineum was lacerated; that there was extensive ulceration of the labia, extending into the rectum; laceration of the genitals, the hymen ruptured, and a purulent discharge from the vagina. She was treated for syphilis, as it was discovered that the prisoner had warty excrescences on the penis, and also syphilitic sores. Mortification set in on the 29th, and she died on the 5th November, thirteen days after the alleged connexion. On the 7th a post-mortem examination was made, when the following appearances were noted:— Mortification of the genitals, extending downwards and backwards to the sacrum. The whole of the soft parts in the genital region, including the urethra, labia, and vaginal orifice, were mortified to the depth of two inches; the rectum and nates were also mortified; the external surface of the bladder showed several patches of inflammation, and its lining membrane was coated with purulent matter. The whole mucous lining of the vagina was black with mortification."

Fortified with the answers received, I addressed the following letter to the Judge:—

"*Dublin, January* 30, 1858.

"My Lord,—I beg to acknowledge the receipt of your note of the 23rd ultimo; I have also been favoured with the perusal of your letter to Mr. Lawrence; I have likewise had communications with Mr. Cobbett, the prisoner's counsel; and have received the depositions of the witnesses in the case of Amos Greenwood. I have, in addition, addressed a circular to, and received answers from, some of the most eminent physicians, surgeons, and medical jurists in the kingdom, respecting this case; and from the investigations I have made, I feel more and more convinced that Mary Johnson *died from natural causes, neither the result of violence nor syphilis*. In endeavouring to make this plain to your Lordship, I labour under the same disabilities which a lawyer would in making me understand the bearings of a legal argument. In both cases the mind requires to be prepared by previous application to the subject, and your Lordship may not have a medical, as I may not possess a legal, mind.

"Your Lordship lays much stress upon the assumed fact that 'the private parts of the child were extensively lacerated, and the perineum ruptured;' and that 'she made no complaint for some days.' On the first of these points I would respectfully join issue with your Lordship, or, more properly speaking, with the evidence adduced to support that allegation. The perineum, or the septum which divides the vagina and anus, it should be remembered, is an exceedingly sensitive part, highly endowed with nerves, and so very vascular that a solution of its continuity must be attended with considerable hemorrhage and exquisite pain. Some accoucheurs, men particularly versed in the anatomy and pathology of this part, declare that it could not be ruptured by the penis in a girl between nine and ten years of age, healthy and well formed as the deceased; while those who believe that it might ‘possibly’ be ruptured give it as their opinion that it is a most unlikely and improbable case. Granting, however, the possibility of this frightful laceration, in which the vagina and rectum must have been thrown into one, I fearlessly assert—and in this opinion I am supported by the highest authorities in Great Britain—that unless it can be shown that Mary Johnson was at the time under the influence of a narcotic or an anæsthetic, she must have given expression to her feelings in loud cries, could scarcely have helped resisting violently, and must have bled profusely.

"Now, I am told it was sworn before your Lordship by Mrs. Handcock, who, with her husband and child, slept in the same room, within one yard of the prisoner, that the deceased made no complaint whatever during the night, nor when she went into the room, twenty minutes or half an hour after the prisoner had retired to bed; and that neither before nor after she went to bed did she hear any cries or struggle; moreover, it appears that this Mrs. Handcock, the child's mistress, swore that she and Greenwood ‘slept that night on *clean sheets*, which she (Mrs. Handcock) rolled up on Friday morning, to bring to Wigan, and *saw nothing on them;* made the bed, on Friday, in a booth in Wigan, and saw nothing; the same on Saturday, Sunday, and Monday.’

"Now, my Lord, I again assert, that if Mary Johnson was torn and lacerated to the extent that was asserted at the trial, and which you evidently believe, there must have been considerable hemorrhage, and the sheets must have exhibited some marks of it. On Tuesday, four days after the alleged assault, some bloody spots were observed on the sheets of the same bed in the booth at Wigan; but then, my Lord, I am given to understand, and it was so stated by witnesses in court, that Greenwood had not slept with Mary Johnson upon the three previous nights. Furthermore, these blood-stains were discovered only after the diseased state of the child had been observed, and she had been examined by a medical man. Mr. Cobbett has written to me to say that Mrs. Handcock proved distinctly that both prisoner and deceased slept in night-clothes, and says —‘ his clothes might have been got rid of: at all events, there was no evidence about the state of his shirt, but there was about the child's night-shift, viz., *that no blood or stains were observed on it.'*

" Supposing, again, that all this violence had been perpetrated, it is my opinion, and the opinion of all practical men acquainted with the subject, that the deceased child could not have risen the next morning, and proceeded about her ordinary business during that and the two following days, travelling from place to place,—certainly not without making some complaint as to her state. It should be remembered that in cases where the perineum is completely ruptured, as occurs occasionally in child-bearing, there is usually incontinence of fæces, a symptom which it would have been scarcely possible to conceal, and which must have attracted the attention of those about the deceased. There was no evidence whatever as to a *recent* laceration; and upon the fifth day, when seen by Mr. Jameson, who is said to be an assistant of Mr. Pickford, a surgeon at Heywood, it is quite manifest, from the state of ' ulceration, sloughing, and mortification' she was in, that he could not then say whether the destruction of the perineum was the result of *laceration* or *ulceration*. With respect to this gentleman's testimony, I beg to append an extract from Mr. Cobbett's letter:—' He said that there had been much violence to the parts, and much laceration, also a vaginal discharge; but did not satisfactorily show whether the discharge arose from clap or syphilis: he said it was *venereal*, and, in his opinion, *gonorrhœa might degenerate into syphilis.'*

" Now, my Lord, I know nothing of the age, experience, or qualifications of Mr. Jameson; but I can assure your Lordship that if such an answer were given by a student when being examined for his diploma in surgery, he ought not to receive his license. From inquiries I have recently made, I cannot find that this gentleman belongs to any College of Physicians or Surgeons in Great Britain or Ireland; and I am given to understand that he is, or has been, a druggist at Heywood, and occasionally assists Mr. Pickford; but I presume your Lordship inquired as to the *qualifications to practise* as well as his pathological acquirements for making a post-mortem examination when receiving his testimony in a case of life and death, and in a matter requiring a combination of practical as well as medico-legal knowledge of more than the ordinary description.

" Mr. Pickford, the surgeon whose assistant Mr. Jameson was said to be, did not attend the child till shortly before her death, when it was impossible for him to say (if the account which I have received of her state then be true) what was the remote or original cause of her death. It is stated that the child was treated for syphilis. If that treatment consisted in the administration of mercury, every person conversant with that disease will tell your Lordship that such treatment was more likely to hasten her death than to promote her cure. With respect to the syphilitic infection, there has not been, in any of the original reports or depositions attributed to Mr. Pickford or Mr. Jameson, all of which are now before me, the slightest attempt at defining the character of the sores. All that is stated is that the genital organs were in a state of 'ulceration, sloughing, and mortification.' But these symptoms do not necessarily form syphilis because they happen to be seated on the female organs of generation. Moreover, it is asserted that when first seen by Mr. Jameson on the fifth day, 'there was extensive ulceration of the labia and along the perineum to the rectum, and a purulent discharge from the vagina.' Now, on the one hand, this purulent discharge is a symptom of gonorrhœa, leucorrhœa, vaginitis, and noma pudendi, but not of syphilis; and the best authorities upon this latter disease assert that the state of ulceration (which, from its extensive nature, must have been in progress for at least a couple of days before Mr. Jameson saw her, and, consequently, bearing date from the third day after the alleged connexion) is incompatible with the known laws of syphilitic affections. With respect to the prisoner, all I can learn is that, on being examined by Mr. Jameson on the 29th of October, 'he had warty excrescences on the penis, and beneath the prepuce syphilitic sores.' This is, however, rather against the probability of his being able, without very great pain to himself, to have had forcible connexion with the deceased.

"Your Lordship states that 'the Jury were satisfied that her (the child's) story was true as to the *fact* of the prisoner having had connexion with her;' but the Jury had no opportunity of seeing the child—I will not say cross-examined, but properly questioned on this matter. And while upon this subject I beg to refer you to the facts set forth upon the various trials related in my work upon 'Infantile Leucorrhœa,' and in particular to Sir A. Cooper's opinion, which I have quoted at length in the preface—see pp. 9, 10, where he used the expression that 'a multitude of persons have been hanged by such a mistake' as that which I believe has been made in the case of Mary Johnson. The child met her mother the next morning (23rd October), and said nothing about the frightful injury she had suffered the night before. Neither did she mention it to Mrs. Handcock, with whom she lived for three days, nor, in fact, to any one, until her state was remarked by a woman named Butterworth ; and according to the report given of the trial, it was two days after this when she stated that violence had been offered her.   But whether such statement was made as the result of leading questions of the women by whom she was surrounded, as is almost invariably the case, or a voluntary declaration on the child's part, did not appear to the public; certain it is, that the moment the mother, friend, or attendant of a child discovers an irritation or any discharge upon the genitals, she almost invariably and immediately jumps to the conclusion that the child has been ' meddled with by a man,' and not only interrogates the child to that effect, but often either persuades her into the belief of the crime, or punishes her until she confesses to an act that has never been committed.   These opinions are not founded on isolated cases, neither are they new; they are perfectly well known to the medical profession, and besides the instances related by myself, numbers of such cases have been recorded during the last thirty years.   In all the fictitious cases that I have known, the disease has been discovered by a *second* party, and the accusation brought out by a series of stereotyped questions, which have remained almost the same from the days when Cooper wrote until now.

"I have just received a letter from Mr. Cobbett, and in answer to my question respecting the way in which the information was first obtained from the child, he writes:—'The child at first *denied* that anything had been done to her, on their asking if some lad had been putting his hand up her coats;' after this, they told her they ' *would not be able to give her any-thing to do her good*,' or to that effect, unless she told the truth. And again, according to a report of the case sent me by Mr. Winnard, the first surgeon who saw her, the women about her 'asked her if any boy had been playing with her? She said, No. Any one putting his hand up her clothes? She said, No. Then they said, *if she did not tell the truth, she would die, that nothing could be got to ease her, and she would be worse*, &c. That she then said Amos Greenwood had on the Thursday night been upon her, and hurt her very much.'   Here I respectfully submit there was both a *suggestion*, a *promise*, and a *threat*, after the usual form ' in such cases made and provided,' a threat that she would be allowed to die unless she accused some one!   This is all I can learn now of the interrogations, but how much further these questions were pressed, or what names were suggested, I know not. I firmly believe, however, that but for these suggestions and threats, the child would have died, and *made no accusation of any one.* No doubt, this did not appear in evidence. Who at the trial was to ask such a question? Even if such a fact were elicited, it is possible that the Jury might not have appreciated it—it would alone have been for the astute mind of a Judge to have seen and valued the bearings of such a statement, if true. Moreover, I would respectfully put it to your Lordship that this child had no object in concealing from her parents or mistress the frightful state of laceration— her vagina torn and bleeding, her perineum ruptured and split into the rectum—when she *was neither influenced by love, passion, nor fear.* Had the prisoner lacerated to the same extent any other portion of her body, I ask your Lordship, not merely as a judge in law, but as a judge of human nature, whether she would have concealed the fact for four days, until compelled to go to bed by the agony she was suffering?

" I have been informed by Mr. Winnard, that on their taxing Greenwood with the perpetration of the crime, he went to the girl directly, denied it, and asked for a police-officer to be sent for.

"In those cases to which I drew public attention some years ago, and which I had the honour of submitting to your Lordship, the disease which caused the false accusations to be made was not of a fatal character, and therefore not applicable in every respect to the case of Mary Johnson. Permit me, therefore, to call your attention to the following. In this same town of Manchester (to which the parties in the present instance belong) a precisely similar case occurred in the year 1791. A child aged four years was discovered by her mother to have her female organs highly inflamed, sore, and painful; ' the child had slept two or three nights in the same bed (says the Report) with a boy fourteen years old, and had complained of having been hurt by him in the night.' The child died of the disease ten days after it was discovered—about the same period as in the case of Mary Johnson. Mr. Ward, a most distinguished surgeon, then attached to the Manchester Infirmary, attended the deceased, upon whom a coroner's inquest was held. He has left the following record, which may be found in the earlier editions of Dr. Percival's Medical Ethics, and has been frequently referred to in works on medical jurisprudence, and also in those on the diseases of women and children, both home and foreign:—' The circumstances above related having been *proved to the satisfaction of the Jury,* and being corroborated by the opinion I gave, that *the child's death was occasioned by external violence,* a verdict of Murder was returned against the boy with whom she had slept.' In the interval between the inquest at Manchester and the trial at Lancaster, several other *fatal* cases occurred from a similar affection, and, to the lasting credit of this truthful man, he thus writes:—' I was then convinced I *had been mistaken* in attributing Jane Harrison's death to external violence, and I informed the coroner of the reasons which produced this change of opinion.' When the case came on for trial, this fact was stated to the Judge, who observed to the Jury, ' that he therefore hoped they would acquit the prisoner without calling any witnesses; with this request the Jury immediately complied.' Since then I have not been able to discover that any other person has been tried in England for the murder of a child by rape, or rape and disease conjointly, until this trial before your Lordship on the 5th of December last[a].

" The next medical account of this disease is styled—' A History of a very fatal Affection of the Pudendum in female Children,' by Mr. Kinder Wood, surgeon in Oldham, and which was communicated by the late Mr. Abernethy to the Medico-Chirurgical Society of London in 1815. This paper has been published in the records of that Society, and I have requested Mr. Lawrence to lend your Lordship a copy of that work, should you desire to see it. In Mr. Wood's cases all the symptoms described in Mary Johnson's case are graphically set forth; and out of twelve instances which he records, ten proved fatal. Indeed, he says—' that when the ulceration is deep and extensive, *I have never seen the patient recover;*' and again:—' I have seen the inflammation spread over the mons veneris, and be succeeded by deep ulceration, progressively increasing as long as life continued; the external organs of generation are now *progressively destroyed,*' &c. In one case ' the perineum was inflamed and covered with aphthæ, which also incrusted the anus; the discharge was thin, copious, and offensive, and had *inflamed the top of the thigh,* where it had been suffered to remain. It is a very remarkable fact that in nearly all the cases of this disease, or of simple vaginitis, one of the earliest symptoms, and that which for obvious reasons soonest attracts

[a] In Ireland I know of but one case of death from rape upon a child, and it arose from that popular superstition, still unhappily prevalent among the ignorant, not only in the British Isles, but also in other parts of the world,—that sexual diseases in the male (gonorrhœa or syphilis) may be cured by having intercourse with a virgin. In the year 1840 a soldier violated an infant eleven months old, and she died the next day. Yet in that case, although the cavity of the abdomen was laid open, the perineum was not quite ruptured. See London Medical Gazette, vol. xxvi p. 160.

attention, is the excoriated state of the inside of the thighs. Now I find in Mrs. Handcock's original depositions the following statement:—'On Sunday night (25th), at Wigan, Mary Johnson, in the *prisoner's presence* at the Crawford Arms, said to me that her thighs smarted.' But smarting of the thighs from excoriation, the very first symptoms worn to in this case, *is no sign of rape or of syphilis.* Moreover, I submit that the child's openly stating, in the prisoner's presence, the cause of her distress, without making any accusation against him at the time, and her denying for three days after that any one had connexion with her, is incompatible with the truth of the subsequent accusation, at least it would be so to medical minds. In Case II., related by Wood, the perineum was particularly affected; the disease extended round the anus; and the open surfaces were deep and foul, secreting largely a thin, offensive matter. These were the only two cases seen early enough to be benefited by treatment.

"Now, my Lord, let me call your special attention to the following paragraph, by the same acute observer of disease and human nature, upwards of forty years ago:—'There is one point of view in which a consideration of the disease is highly important. The instances in which parents, on behalf of their children, bring forward individuals upon the charge of rape are *disgustingly frequent; and it can be scarcely doubted that this disease has been frequently considered in court as evidence of violence and venereal infection; inflammation, ulceration, and discharge,* having had always *particular attention* in a consideration of the evidence.' I regret to say, these cases, so pertinent to that of the trial at Liverpool, and these truthful remarks, which one would imagine had been elicited by the case of Mary Johnson, do not appear in the prominent light in which they should in the last edition of the only English work on Medical Jurisprudence to which lawyers and medical men now refer, although they are to be found in works published in other countries.

" Now if the medical man and his assistant, who saw this case, in what must be acknowledged an advanced stage, were not acquainted with these cases related by Percival and Kinder Wood, I respectfully submit they were not adequate witnesses; and were as likely to be mistaken, with respect to the true nature of this affection, as Mr. Ward was sixty-seven years ago, or as the surgeon described by Sir A. Cooper in his Lecture on the subject, or as the London practitioner mentioned by Mr. Lawrence in his letter to me in 1853, published at page 24 of my tract,—to which letter I would the more particularly direct your Lordship's attention, because you will there find that the Judge who presided at the Old Bailey when the case was tried read during the trial this very paper of Mr. Kinder Wood's in the Medico-Chirurgical Transactions, but with which it does not appear that any one connected with the prosecution, defence, or trial of Greenwood was acquainted.

" As soon as I was informed of the names of the medical witnesses, I wrote to Mr. Pickford of Heywood, and to Mr. Winnard of Wigan. From the former gentleman I particularly wished to know, what was the treatment employed by him and Mr. Jameson, in the case of Mary Johnson; and also whether either of them was acquainted with the instances mentioned in the Medico-Chirurgical Transactions above alluded to, and the disease described by Kinder Wood, and which is now generally known by the name of *Noma Pudendi.*

" Mr. Winnard, of Wigan, who first saw the child after her state was discovered, and who *must* have observed the rupture of the perineum and laceration of the vagina, if such existed at this time, no matter how trivial his examination, has afforded me the following history of his knowledge of this case, as well as of the evidence which he gave at the trial:—' Two women brought Mary Johnson to me on Monday morning, the 26th of October, and said they wanted something for the little girl, who was very sore. *I opened the labia;* the parts were inflamed, inside livid; lips swelled, and had *ulcerated spots all over*, varying in size from that of a pea downwards, and covered with yellowish-white sloughs. I ordered her some black wash and a purgative powder. In the afternoon of the same day one of the women came to me and asked could swallowing a sixpence cause such a sore. The answer was, ' Certainly not;' and that the girl was very ill, and required care. Several days afterwards a police-officer came from Heywood and asked me to give a certificate as to what was the matter with the girl: this I refused, nothing having been said to induce me to be minute in my examination. The next I heard was when a policeman came and subpœna'd me to the Assizes, saying that mortification came on, the girl died, and a man was in custody charged with a rape upon her. At the trial I said I made but a slight examination, but considered the case one of *severe vaginitis* when I saw it; *that there was nothing said to me on either the first or second occasion that I saw these people about violation.* That when they were in Wigan they lived in a very dirty, foul place, called the " Pig Market;" and that in that yard I had then a severe case of vaginitis, which had only been arrested by repeated applications of lunar caustic. That I thought syphilitic virus coming in contact with a mucous membrane abraded might induce such symptoms as I saw on the child; and that I thought vaginitis might pass into ulceration and mortification; but that I believed such a disease was more common from two to five years of age.' This evidence, I respectfully submit, should have been sufficient, if properly placed before the Jury, to show them that on the Monday after the alleged offence, and *prior to any accusation* being made, the child was labouring under a well-known disease peculiar to her age and condition of life; and that she did not exhibit any sign of having suffered from violence three days before. From the foregoing recital it appears to me utterly impossible that Mr. Winnard could have overlooked even a partial rupture of the perineum, if such then existed. It is, however, quite compatible with the usual rapid nature of the disease, that the sloughing and ulcerative process may have so far advanced in a day or two, that a person not acquainted with such diseases might mistake it (especially when he was *told* that a rape had been perpetrated) for the result of violence. Mr. Winnard was not present at the post-mortem examination, which I think he should have been.

" I also received answers from Messrs. Pickford and Jameson. The former gentleman says :—' *I must confess that I was not aware of the fatal cases to which you allude in your letter when I was examined at the trial; nor even yet have I seen any description of them;* so that I cannot say whether Mary Johnson's appearance in any way resembled them or not.' This is the more remarkable, as the disease is described (almost in the terms employed by Messrs. Pickford and Jameson) at page 602 of the ' Surgeon's Vade Mecum,' by Mr. Druitt, the seventh edition, which is, I believe, in the hands of nearly every surgeon in Great Britain and Ireland.

" Although your Lordship has already heard Mr. Pickford's statement, I beg leave to append, from his manuscript, the following very characteristic report, which he says is the evidence that he gave both at the inquest and on the trial:—' When I first saw Mary Johnson, which was on the 30th of October, 1857, I found that *mortification* of the upper part of her genitals had then commenced, and there was *an extensive phagedenic ulcer* on the lower part of her genitals, spreading towards the nates. I again saw her on the 1st of November, when the whole of the soft parts between the pubes and the sacrum appeared to be in a state of mortification. On my third and last visit, which was on the 4th of November, *the skin of her nates had disappeared* to the extent of several inches, and had left the cellular tissue completely bare and black. She died on the 5th; and on the 7th Mr. Taylor, the Union Surgeon for this township, Mr. Jameson, and myself, made a post-mortem examination of her body: when we found a mortification of her genitals that extended from the pubes downwards, and as far backwards and upwards as the sacrum. The whole of her genitals, including the mons veneris, labia pudendi, urethra, and vaginal orifice, were a complete mass of mortification; the anus, rectum, and nates, were in a similar state of mortification to a great depth; on opening the abdomen and removing the pubes, we found the bladder quite empty, and rather inflamed externally, but internally there were numerous patches of inflammation, and the whole of its mucous lining was covered with thin purulent matter. The whole of the lining membrane of the vagina was black through mortification; but the uterus did not exhibit any unnatural appearances.'

" So far, so good. Let this very proper description be handed to any jury of scientific medical men, and they will at once decide that Mary Johnson died of *noma pudendi*. However, Mr. Pickford adds the following, which I fearlessly assert was not warranted by the foregoing appearances, either in life or after death, had not his mind been prejudiced by the previous statement that a rape had been committed:—' The conclusion that we came to was—that the immediate cause of Mary Johnson's death was mortification of her genitals; which mortification was the consequence of an inflammation that must have been produced either by extreme violence, or by venereal poison, or most probably by both.'

" Mr. Jameson's statement it is unnecessary to quote at length, except so far as it bears upon the direct question at issue. He says that, having been first told by Betty Handcock, on October 27th, that Mary Johnson ' had been assaulted by Amos Greenwood, on the Thursday night previous, I proceeded up to the bed-room, where she was lying in bed; I then asked her, previous to examining her person, to tell me all about the affair, and the *truth*. She began by saying that, some time during the Thursday night, she awoke and *found Amos Greenwood lying upon her*, and that he had put his ' fie-for-shame' into hers; that he kept moving about upon her, she thought, about *half an hour;* she frequently told him to get off her, but he still continued ; and that just before he did so, all at once he gave her great pain, and she felt as if she had been cut open with a knife."

" From this we learn that Mr. Jameson, instead of proceeding, as a medical man, to examine the person of the child, began by inquiring into the legal history of the case, and, therefore, *preparing* himself for finding a laceration of the genitals before he had been taught even the anatomy of these parts.  We also learn a most important fact, which I would particularly press upon your Lordship's attention, that, according to Mr. Jameson's statement, the child awoke by finding the prisoner 'lying upon her,' and that he remained ' half an hour' in that position; therefore, the act must have been committed long *after* the Handcocks, *who occupied a bed which was sworn* in evidence to˙have been *within one yard* of that occupied by the prisoner and the deceased, had retired to rest!  Does your Lordship believe that this act could have been so committed without the screams and struggles of the child being heard by her mistress, who was within a few feet of her, and to whom she could appeal when she felt ' as if cut open with a knife'[a].

"The remaining portion of Mr. Jameson's evidence is, that the prisoner Greenwood was sent for to the booth, when ' *he, of course, denied it;*' and that, when he examined him, he 'found the prepuce covered with warty excrescences, and on the glans were several sores, from which there was a very offensive discharge.'  This is the first time I have heard or read of a ' *very offensive* discharge' from venereal sores on the glans penis, except in cases of sloughing or ulceration, which it is manifest was in this instance utterly impossible: but the expression here used by Mr. Jameson tallies with the ' *offensive discharge*,' the result of mortification in the child said to be the object of the prisoner's assault.

"The medical portion of the case is thus described by this gentleman:—' I found the organs of generation externally swollen and very much inflamed, *and here and there small ulcers;* from the vagina came a very profuse sanious discharge; she was suffering great pain, the perineum being lacerated. I was able to pass my fingers easily up to the uterus, the hymen being also ruptured; the discharge had inflamed the surrounding parts.'  The small ulcers here and there were the aphthous sores described by the various authors who have written on this disease, but neither the result of rape nor syphilis. As to the perineum being *lacerated*, it is quite manifest that it would not be possible even for an educated practitioner to state whether the rent he *then saw* was the result of *ulceration* or

---

[a] " In the second explanatory depositions of Mrs. Handcock, after the child's death, which are now before me, she says, ' I asked [the child] why she did not call out ? and she said she shamed.'  And thus, if the evidence be true respecting the ruptured perineum, she suffered the most excruciating agony when she might have relieved herself by calling to her mistress."

*laceration.* His treatment consisted in the immediate use of mercury for the three following days, until Mr. Pickford was called in, who most properly ordered the mercury to be discontinued, and quina to be given instead.

"Mr. Pickford thus alludes to his assistant's knowledge of the case:—'It was, I believe, on the 28th October when Mr. Jameson first mentioned Mary Johnson's case to me ; and in giving a description of it he said that on his first examination he found laceration of the girl's perineum, and that her genitals had, in consequence of the laceration, an appearance exactly like the opening that is made in a pig's throat by a butcher when he kills it; consequently, Mary Johnson's case could not at the commencement be noma pudendi.' Now Mr. Jameson in his information swore, that when he *first* saw her, she had extensive ulceration from the labia and perineum up to the rectum. She was suffering from venereal disease; from syphilis; there was *ulceration from the mons veneris to the rectum!* Certainly the incisions made by our butchers in Ireland never exhibit any such appearances.

"There are two subjects suggested to me by the foregoing depositions, one of which must, no doubt, have struck your Lordship at the trial. It is, the state of demoralization of the people with whom the deceased lived, who put her and the prisoner to sleep in the same bed!—an act on which your Lordship, no doubt, animadverted at the time the case came before you. The other circumstance is that, no matter whether the symptoms were the result of violence, syphilis, or noma, the use of mercury was equally improper.

"In a case of this kind, when a man was to have been tried for his life for a very rare offence, a country surgeon and his assistant, no matter how valuable they might be as practitioners in their neighbourhood, are about as competent to decide as I, or any other surgeon or physician not specially instructed therein, would be to determine in a case of poisoning, requiring great medico-legal knowledge, and the subtle chemical analysis, requisite for such investigations.

"With respect to the defence of the prisoner, it was in reality no defence. I learn from the 'Times' that 'Mr. Cobbett, assigned by the Court, defended the prisoner.' If such assignment is similar to that practised in this country, I have reason to know it is often done at the moment of trial, when the junior barrister to whom the case is given knows nothing of the circumstances of it, has no brief, has not had time to look up the legal points which might be urged on the prisoner's behalf, or to consult medical authorities if such were requisite, but simply endeavours, on the spur of the moment, to break down witnesses by adroit cross-examination, or addresses the Jury either on the improbabilities of the case, if there is room for doubt, or, if the case is clear, by an earnest appeal to their feelings. I would respectfully suggest that if a prisoner is to be defended at the expense of the country, he should be defended properly, or not at all. Had Amos Greenwood been wealthy, he would have had an attorney, and have been defended by counsel previously well prepared, who would probably have brought several of the foregoing circumstances before your Lordship and the Jury in a far more effective manner than I have been able to do; and he might have procured such medical evidence as would have laid before the Court a true statement as to the cause of Mary Johnson's disease and death. And I am fully convinced that, had you heard the evidence of any two or three of the eminent medical men whose opinions I have obtained in this case, and which opinions I herewith submit for your Lordship's perusal, you would have either directed the Jury to acquit the prisoner, or to give him the benefit of any doubt which might arise in their minds, respecting the true cause of her death.

"Few criminal lawyers are sufficiently versed in medical jurisprudence as to be able to take up a case upon either side of a question without previously 'making up;' and even then they are likely to be mistaken on the most trivial technicalities. Now, my Lord, in this trial for murder at Liverpool, no one in court seems to have been aware of the possibility of the disease having been mistaken by the medical men, of the likelihood of the child's having died from spontaneous disease, and of the common occurrence of children being, under such circumstances, induced to make false accusations. Moreover, independent of the difficulty which a lawyer has in defending such a case, so put to him, there is invariably a prejudice against the prisoner; from the nature of the offence, there is naturally a public outcry against its atrocity, and the female portion of the community are loud in their cries for vengeance.

" Besides the difficulties under which I labour in bringing this case before your Lordship, and to which I have alluded in the commencement of this letter, I also feel that medical evidence, however truthful, coming from the highest authority, and based either on the acknowledged principles of science or extended observation and experience, has not the same weight with a large proportion of the Bar as a statement made respecting an *alleged* fact by a non-medical witness. Among the many causes which have induced this scepticism, not the least prominent is that of sueh instanees as oeeurred in the case of the trial of Amos Greenwood. But the Bar and the public might as well eavil at the legal opinion of an attorney's elerk, if offered on a ease of law, as at the evidenee of a ehemist and druggist, who had no opportunity of aequiring a knowledge of disease either by lectures, hospital attendanee, or personal ex-perienee.

"I have now but to thank your Lordship for the courtesy and attention you have given to my eommunieations, and to direet your attention to the answers of the queries I addressed on the case to some of my professional brethren, and who, with two ex-ceptions (upon which I have eommented in the proper plaee) are all in favour of the girl having died of disease arising without sexual intereourse. I should add that, although this case in-volves several medieo-legal points, an experieneed practical physician or surgeon is more likely to arrive at a eorrect con-clusion than a mere medieo-legal jurist. Your Lordship will therefore perceive, that the persons from whom I sought infor-mation are engaged in the practieal branches of the profession.

"Should it turn out that this horrid erime, of whieh the ae-eused has been found guilty, was not eommitted, I need not tell your Lordship that it will be a source of satisfaetion to the sur-viving friends of the deeeased. My ehief desire is, that this ease may not hereafter be created into a preeedent; and even al-though I may not have sueceeded in convineing your Lordship, I have the satisfaetion of having done my duty to my profession. Should, however, your Lordship be now of opinion that a mis-take may have been committed in this ease, your high sense of justiee will, I feel assured, lead you to permit me to take such steps as will tend to its reetification.

"With respect to the prisoner, I have, as your Lordship is aware, no interest in his present state; if he is a well-conducted man, it may be an improvement on his late condition,—that of a costermonger's assistant. My interferenee is not on *his* be-half, but in what I eonsider to be the eause of truth, justice, and medical scienee.

"The following is the list of queries sent, together with the statement, given at page 54, to the medieal men, whose opinions are appended thereto. The original documents have been all earefully preserved, and ean be forwarded to your Lordship, if neeessary,"

### QUERIES.

"I. Is rupture of the perineum likely to have been pro-dueed after the mannner deseribed; or have you known any eases of forced connexion in whieh it oceurred?

" II. The fact of the ruptured perineum, in the forced connexion, was laid great stress upon by the Judge. Do you think the perineum could have been ruptured after the manner described, without the child resisting, and giving expression to her feelings in loud cries, sufficient to awaken the three other persons who slept in the same room with her?

" III. Would hemorrhage sufficient to mark the child's night-dress, and the sheets, follow a rupture of the perineum in forced connexion; and if such a sign was absent, what inference would you draw therefrom?

" IV. If the perineum was ruptured, and the vagina and neighbouring parts lacerated to the extent described five days afterwards, do you think she could have risen next morning, and proceeded to her work as usual, not making any complaint to her parents or mistress until her state was observed three days afterwards?

" V. Does syphilis ever in the female child assume the form described, on the fourth day after connexion?

" VI. Do you know any disease likely to arise spontaneously, which presents the appearances described in the foregoing statement, and which is likely to end fatally?

" VII. What amount of credence is to be attached to the evidence of children with respect to connexion, when the suspicious appearances are discovered several days after the supposed act?

" VIII. To what would you attribute the death of Mary Johnson?"

The answers to these questions have been arranged according to the order in which they were received: the Roman numerals correspond to those prefixed to the Queries.

From Alfred M'Clintock, M.D., F.R.C.S.I., Master of the Lying-in Hospital, Dublin:—

" I. I do *not* think it possible for the perineum to have been ruptured in the manner described; nor have I ever known or heard of a case where forced connexion produced this result.

" II. My answer to this query is already given.

" III. I think that forced connexion, sufficient to rupture the perineum, would, supposing the female to be in bed, cause a hemorrhagic stain on her dress, and on the sheets. The absence of any such stain upon her linen I would regard as disproving a forced penetration.

" IV. Quite impossible that she could have done so.

" V. I have never known syphilis, in any stage, produce appearances such as were found at this post-mortem examination; and I do not believe it possible that these appearances were due to the alleged causes.

" VI. Yes; a form of spontaneous gangrene, which spreads rapidly, and occasions extensive destruction of all the contiguous parts.

" VII. None; unless corroborated by direct circumstantial evidence.

" VIII. To noma pudendi, or gangrenous inflammation commencing in the genitals.

" 31st *December,* 1857."

From Fleetwood Churchill, M.D., M.R.I.A., Professor of Midwifery, and the Diseases of Women and Children in the King and Queen's College of Physicians in Ireland, author of a work on " The Diseases of Children:"—

" I. I have known no case of laceration of the perineum produced by forcible connexion, nor do I think such an effect at all likely.

" II. I do not think that the perineum could have been ruptured in the manner supposed, without the severest suffering; and it is not likely that a child of ten years old would have suppressed all expression of pain.

" III. I think rupture of the perineum, from forced connexion, would be *immediately* followed by considerable hemorrhage; the absence of which, to my mind, would be very strong evidence indeed that no such rupture took place.

" IV. If the extent of damage supposed had been inflicted, I do not believe it possible that she could have gone to work as usual without such pain as must inevitably have arrested observation.

" V. I never saw syphilis in females assume the form described in the Report; nor do I believe that the combined effects of rape and syphilis would produce that result.

" VI. You will find, in my 'Diseases of Women,' pp. 52, 53, the description of a disease from Dugès and Kinder Wood, which closely resembles the post-mortem description you have sent me. It is gangrenous ulceration of the genitals; and if I were to give an opinion, I should say that it was this disease of which the child died.

" VII. Little or no weight, unless the disclosure is voluntary, and made within a very short period. None at all, if the mother has catechised the child, for she is sure to put leading questions which indicate to the child what she is to say.

" VIII. As I have said, to gangrenous ulceration of the female genitals, extending into the pelvis.

"Let me add one remark. There is not only no evidence of *laceration* of the perineum, but negative evidence that it was not lacerated, for the first medical man who examined her *could not* have overlooked such fearful damage unless he were blind, or did not examine her at all.

"*December* 31*st*, 1857."

Upon the subject of syphilis alone I have received the following note from Thomas Byrne, F.R.C.S.I., Surgeon to the Lock Hospital, Dublin:—

"In reply to your note of yesterday, I have to assure you that I have never seen, in young or old, a fatal case of primary syphilis, attended with sloughing, ulceration, and mortification of the genitals; we have, however, from time to time, many cases in the Lock of sloughing primary sores, occurring generally in very young women."

From William Lawrence, F.R.S., Surgeon Extraordinary to the Queen; Surgeon to St. Bartholomew's Hospital; author of an essay on "A peculiar Affection of the Genitals in Female Children," &c. &c.:—

"I. I have neither known nor heard of any instance in which the perineum has been ruptured by forcible attempts at sexual intercourse with a female at any age.

"II. Assuming, what I hardly believe to be possible, that the perineum could be ruptured by an attempt at forcible connexion, there would be severe pain, and such outcries as *could not fail* to awaken and alarm persons sleeping in the same room.

"III. If the perineum could be ruptured in forced connexion, which I doubt, or if the parts should be lacerated in a similar attempt, I believe that sufficient bleeding would necessarily follow to mark the night-dress of the child, and to appear on the sheets. In the absence of such signs, I should infer that neither rupture nor laceration had taken place.

"IV. If the perineum had been ruptured, and the vagina and neighbouring parts lacerated to the extent mentioned as having been observed five days afterwards, she could not possibly have risen next morning and proceeded to her work without complaint, and still less have continued to do so for three days.

"V. Syphilis never assumes the form described on the fourth day after connexion, either in the child or the adult. The symptoms described are altogether unlike those of syphilis, which seldom shows itself earlier than from the seventh to the tenth day after infection, and then in a form little calculated to alarm.

" VI. Female children are liable to a peculiar inflammation of the genital organs, sometimes proceeding rapidly to foul ulceration, and even mortification. *In some instances death has been caused by this affection within a few days. I attribute the death of Mary Johnson to this disease.*

" VII. I believe that very little reliance can be placed on the evidence of young children, when, in addition to serious illness, they have been alarmed by accusations and threats, and teased by repeated questionings.

" *1st January,* 1858."

From Thomas Geoghegan, M. D., F. R. C. S. I., Professor of Medical Jurisprudence in the Royal College of Surgeons in Ireland; Surgeon to the City of Dublin Hospital:—

" I. Rupture of the perineum (in the anatomical sense of the word), as an attendant on defloration, is rare, although I am aware of cases both recorded and otherwise. Its occurrence would be, obviously, more likely, *cæteris paribus*, in the young than in the adult subject, although I have reason to believe that it is not confined to the former.

" As respects the case now submitted, I confess the medical evidence does not appear to me unequivocally to substantiate the fact of rupture of the perineum, or even of the hymen; for when the examination was made (on the sixth day), it appears that there was 'extensive ulceration of the labia, extending into the rectum' (and hence through the perineum?), a condition *likely* to render the verification of either form of rupture difficult or *impossible at the date assigned.* It seems further very improbable that a person described as labouring under venereal 'in its most virulent form,' should be physically capable of inflicting a degree of violence sufficient to lacerate the perineum. If, however, the accused had succeeded in doing so, laceration on the surface of the male organ might reasonably have been expected. This, however, is not noted among the appearances discovered[a].

" II. If the perineum or part of the recto-vaginal septum had been ruptured, as described, I should have expected that the assault would have been discovered by those in the same apartment, unless the cries of the sufferer were forcibly suppressed; or that the occurrence would have betrayed itself very soon

---

[a] Mr. Jameson, the only person who examined the prisoner, states that he had *venereal warts*, a condition rendering rupture of the perineum more difficult, and, taken in connexion with the foregoing opinion of Professor Geoghegan, almost impossible, without great pain, and perhaps hemorrhage from the penis.

afterwards, either by incapacity for motion, or at least by alteration of gait and manner.

" III. IV. & V. Certainly; even rupture of the hymen, unaccompanied by any injury of the perineum, is usually attended by hemorrhage, which, in one case that fell under my observation, was so copious as to demand surgical interference. Considering the disparity of the adult male organ to that of a girl of the age stated, the absence of blood on the clothes, presuming the garments not to have been interfered with, would, in my opinion, render forcible penetration most improbable, and rupture of the perineum, I think, impossible. The progress and termination of the local mischief were unlike those of defloration, whether the latter be accompanied or not by venereal infection. Under the circumstances, it is to the last degree unlikely that sphacelus would have been the result of defloration only; whilst its occurrence to the degree and in the form assigned, as the consequence of venereal infection, is witnessed in the female sex only in persons addicted to gross intemperance, of broken-down habit, and usually the subject of ulceration of some standing. The progress of the previous ulceration in Johnson's case was equally unlike that usually observed in venereal. On the fourth day after the reputed infection, it had made very considerable advances: at this period, usually, syphilitic virus has either not as yet manifested its local effects, or has made but trivial progress, unless the parts inoculated have been already the seat of some other form of ulceration.

" VI. There is a peculiar and long recognised disease which attacks the genitals of young females, apparently a form of pemphigus gangrenosus, commencing in unhealthy inflammation, and proceeding to ulceration and gangrene, and frequently compromising life. Whether the deceased girl was the subject of a criminal assault or otherwise, I am of opinion that the character of the local symptoms, and the progress and termination of the case, are in conformity with those of the disease above mentioned.

" VII. Speaking without reference to any special case, it is unquestionably matter of experience, that the urgent interference of relatives and friends has often led to statements given in evidence by children, totally irreconcilable with the medical facts.

" *4th January,* 1858."

From William Acton, F.R.C.S., author of a " Treatise on Venereal Affections, including certain Affections of the Uterus," &c., &c., London :—

" I have much pleasure in answering your queries, as I think we should all aid in solving these odd cases in young girls, and rescue the man, if we conscientiously can; for I believe *many have been transported or hanged on imperfect medical evidence.* The case you propose for my opinion is similar to a few I have seen, and I think we can come to a solution of the difficulty.

" I. In answer to the first query, I may confidently state that I never heard or saw, or think it possible, that the genital organ of a man could produce a rupture of the perineum in a girl.

" II. To the second query I answer—No; I think her cries would have raised the sleepers, had such violence been used.

" III. The third question I answer thus—I do not think a girl could have been so injured, and the next morning gone to her work.

" IV. and V. The fourth question, as well as the fifth, may be thus answered:—In the delicate, ill-fed, and badly lodged poor of London, we occasionally find phagedena arising, which is capable of committing the ravages described in the above case. This form of sloughing phagedena has attacked the wards of St. Bartholomew's Hospital last year, so severely that the authorities closed the rooms in which the beds were placed, death having destroyed, I think, three young women from extensive ulceration of the generative organs. This form usually attacks syphilitic cases, and the child in Liverpool may or may not have had the disease. The child is said, I find, to have been treated for syphilis. Was mercury given her? and, if so, did not this further complicate her malady, whatever that may have been. I gave the case of a child brought into St. Bartholomew's Hospital, at page 4 of the Introduction to my second edition, which bears upon this case : had such a case been given mercury, I think we might have seen death followed by all the consequences you detail to me.

" VI. In answer to the sixth query, I should remark that the credence given to children should not be great, nor to the statements of the ' immediate surroundings,' to use an expression Owen employs, unless corroborated by medical probabilities.

" VII. In reply to the seventh query, I say phagedena, or sloughing phagedena, may have produced all the sequelæ; but whether this was superadded on simple ulcers, or syphilis, warts, and purulent discharge, the evidence gave me no clue to decide.

" *4th January,* 1858."

From Alfred S. Taylor, M. D., Professor of Medical Jurisprudence and Chemistry in Guy's Hospital School of Medicine, London; author of " Medical Jurisprudence," &c. :—

" I. Rupture of the perineum may take place under these circumstances :—(Case by Dr. Cheevers, in a girl aged 6, but looking younger—Medical Jurisprudence for India, page 46. Case by Dr. Brady, in a child, aged eleven months, fatal in about twenty hours.—Medical Gazette, vol. xxvi., page 160.)

" II. I think the perineum might be ruptured without the child resisting. One would anticipate crying; but fear might repress this. The cries, if made, might or might not awaken persons sleeping in the same room: that would depend upon circumstances. I find no evidence of resistance or crying in the cases quoted[a].

" III. I certainly cannot comprehend how laceration of the perineum, &c., from violence, could occur without effusion of blood taking place sooner or later. If it could be proved that neither the *sheets* nor the *linen* worn on that night by the child was bloody, this would be a strong point against the laceration having been produced at that time in the manner suggested; and that antecedent and other causes might have been concerned in the production of the injuries. In my judgment, this would make a case more strongly in favour of the prisoner than any of the other matters which depend upon probability or speculation, and on which professional opinion might be easily divided.

" IV. I should certainly expect that a person whose genitals presented the appearance described on the fifth day would have complained of pain and uneasiness for four or five days before the date of examination, and would have had difficulty in going about her usual work.

" V. No; I have never heard of such a case. It would not account for the purulent discharge or the laceration—i. e. syphilis unaccompanied by gonorrhœa.

" VI. I know of no disease likely to arise spontaneously which would present the appearances described,—e. g. rupture or laceration of the perineum. Vaginitis may arise from spontaneous or mechanical causes: it may be followed by mortification and death. It is not likely to end fatally when depending on ordinary spontaneous causes[b].

" VII. This is a legal question. Children untutored are

---

[a] See remarks on these passages in the next page.

[b] Of the twelve cases recorded by Kinder Wood, all arising from " *spontaneous causes*," ten ended fatally.

considered by lawyers to make excellent witnesses to *facts.* There might be reasons which would induce a child to conceal an act of this kind perpetrated on her, especially if she were a consenting party, or made no resistance in the first instance. I do not see that this fact should alone be sufficient to impeach the veracity of the statement[a].

" VIII. Under all the circumstances, I am inclined to attribute death to inflammation from violence alone to the genital organs. I can perceive no adequate cause for the inflammation and death but this.

" *5th January*, 1858."

The only two cases of ruptured perineum from rape, on record, are, I believe, those referred to by Dr. Taylor[b]. That afforded by Dr. Brady in the Medical Gazette is the instance of the child, eleven months old, to which I have already referred at p. 61; but it bears no analogy to the case of Mary Johnson. The Indian case I have not read the particulars of, and therefore cannot offer any analysis thereof. But Dr. Taylor does not enumerate ruptured perineum among the possible marks of violence described in the present edition of his Medical Jurisprudence[c]. The weight of medical evidence is also against his opinion. With respect to a child not resisting or crying from fear, it is questionable whether she would be able to restrain her feelings, even if influenced by that, or any other motives. In the case of the child eleven months old, what resistance could be offered; and who could hear its cries when, as stated in the Report, the man, with the child in his arms, ' walked on quickly, and was out of sight for half an hour.' I am at a loss to know what are the circumstances that would prevent persons in ordinary sleep hearing a child of ten years of age crying within one yard of them.

As regards the answer to the sixth query, I apprehend that physicians or surgeons who see much of the diseases of children

[a] In answer to this seventh query, Sir Astley Cooper's opinion, and all those writers who have followed in the same course of investigation, seems to have been overlooked. And Dr. Taylor writes thus, upon this subject, in the last edition of his work on Medical Jurisprudence, that of 1858:—"The statement of the child may be simple and artlessly made: at this tender age a girl may be easily induced, by fear of punishment and the aid of leading questions, to admit that some one had committed an assault upon her; the statement, once made, may be persevered in, and *its inconsistency may not be always brought out by cross-examination.*"

[b] Since writing the foregoing, a case occurred in London in which a child, aged 5, was violated by a boy some years older: the perineum was *partially* lacerated ; but she screamed violently, and bled profusely.

[c] That of 1854, the last published when this communication was sent to Sir W. Wightman.

will not agree with Dr. Taylor on the pathology of these affections; and it is totally at variance with Kinder Wood's description of the disease which, although depending on ordinary "spontaneous causes," proved fatal in ten cases out of twelve.

From Thomas Beatty, M. D., F.R.C.S.I., lately Professor of Midwifery, and formerly of Medical Jurisprudence, in the Royal College of Surgeons in Ireland; and author of the article "Rape" in the Cyclopædia of Practical Medicine:—

"I. I think it is possible, but not probable; I never knew a case of it: I recollect a case in which the prisoner split the perincum of a child with a knife.

"II. The violence to effect the supposed rupture must have been so great as to *compel* screaming in the child, sufficient to rouse all in the room.

"III. If the perincum was ruptured in forced connexion, *there must have been* a considerable hemorrhage, and all the clothes of the child and the sheets must have been stained with blood. If such an appearance was not present at the time a rape with such violence was said to have taken place, I would disbelieve the assertion that the crime had been committed.

"IV. I do not believe she could.

"V. I know no form of syphilis that could produce these effects, even if combined with the violence of rape.

"VI. There is a disease well known, and long ago described by Dr. Kinder Wood, which presents all the characters of the disease found in the girl Mary Johnson, and which almost always ends fatally. I have seen it myself, and I have no doubt that the case of this girl was of a similar nature.

"VII. None whatever.

"VIII. To the gangrenous disease above alluded to, totally irrespective of violence.

"11*th January*, 1858."

From J. Y. Simpson, M. D., Professor of Midwifery in the University of Edinburgh:—

"I have read over your statement very carefully, and *I have no doubt whatever in my own mind that Amos Greenwood has been quite erroneously convicted.* The child evidently died of the *non*-venereal affection,—noma or phagedena of the vulva. I am not aware of any modern physician or surgeon having seen, or pretended to see, any variety whatever of venereal disease prove fatal in thirteen days, whilst that is the common end, and about the common course, of pudendal noma, when it occurs spontaneously in childhood. Besides, it is highly improbable that the perineum, &c., could have been so seriously torn and lacerated, as is alleged, in any attempted connexion, without the girl crying out, and without her showing marks of injury in her gait.

"I believe it is very improbable that the laceration of the perineum could be caused by the forcible introduction of the penis into the vagina; but if such was the case, as alleged, I consider that it could not have taken place under the circumstances you describe without causing such exclamations of pain as would rouse the other inmates of the room from their sleep. I believe that the cause of the child's death was noma, or sloughing phagedena of the parts.

" 12*th January*, 1858."

From Sir Benjamin Brodie, Bart., Sergeant Surgeon to the Queen; formerly Surgeon to St. George's Hospital, London:—

"I have carefully read the Report of the trial of Amos Greenwood, as communicated to me by Mr. Wilde. Unless there were really positive signs of the little girl's perineum having been lacerated *by mechanical violence*, I should doubt such an injury having taken place. There is nothing in the symptoms, as I have seen them described, which may not be accounted for as the result of disease; and indeed it seems highly improbable that such violence should have been used as would have lacerated the perineum, without the girl having been heard to scream, and the linen having been stained with blood.

"At the same time, considering—1st, that Greenwood slept in the same bed with the girl; 2ndly, that he had warts and sores on his genital organs; 3rdly, that the girl was affected with symptoms which are not often of spontaneous origin, and which might have been the result of infection, I must say that it seems to me that there is great reason to believe that the charge against the prisoner, so far as his having made attempts to have sexual intercourse with the girl, was not without foundation.

"Further than this, I cannot venture to give an opinion without having before me the details of the evidence offered on the occasion of the trial, including, of course, the examination and cross-examination of the witnesses.

" 20*th January*, 1858."

From John H. Power, M.D., Surgeon to Jervis-street Hospital, and Professor of Practical Anatomy in the Royal College of Surgeons in Ireland:—

"I. I believe that rupture of the perineum is not likely to

occur in the manner described, and to the extent stated, in a child ten years of age. I have never known of the occurrence of such a case. I have had on many occasions the means of ascertaining the size of the orifice of the vagina in very young subjects and infants, and have found it much larger than is generally supposed,—e. g., in a subject three years of age, which died from a burn on the chest, I found the orifice measured, in the vertical diameter, one inch and a quarter fully when dilated; and transversely about one-eighth inch less.

" II. Extensive and forced laceration, such as described, could not, in my opinion, have taken place without resistance on the part of the sufferer, nor without such expressions of pain as would awaken some one or more of these who might have slept in the same room with her.

" III. Were such a rupture or laceration of the external parts, as that described to me, to have taken place from forced connexion, there must have been hemorrhage. If in this case there was no hemorrhage, I think it is quite clear that the child could not have sustained the violence spoken of, but must have died of disease.

" IV. I think it utterly impossible that any child who had sustained an extensive laceration of the perineum, and concomitant injuries of the external organs, could have arisen and gone about her ordinary avocations on the morning following, without enduring the most intense suffering, and manifesting the same to those closely associated with her. I believe a constitutional shock following so severe an injury must have been quite manifest.

" V. From my experience of syphilis in the female, I am not able to afford the necessary information in reply to this question.

" VI. I do know of a disease in this country which frequently presents the appearances described to me, and which frequently terminates fatally. In the Dublin Medical Essays for the year 1807 there is a paper written by the late Dr. Whitley Stokes, on this very disease, and which I find headed thus:—' On an Eruptive Disease of Children;' and in the table of contents and heading:—' Dr. Stokes on *Pemphigus Gangrenosus;*' Dr. Stokes gave the latter name to the disease. He describes it as attacking the genitals, as well as other parts of the body. (See his paper.)

" VII. I have heard of many instances in which children, under circumstances such as those described to me, have made statements, certainly not spontaneously, but under the direction of designing parties; I am, therefore, disposed in such cases to receive these statements, made several days after the supposed act, with extreme caution.

"VIII. Under all the circumstances of the case of Mary Johnson, as described to me, I think her death resulted, in all human probability, from the disease called by Dr. Whitley Stokes, 'pemphigus gangrenosus.'

"24*th January*, 1858."

From W. B. Kesteven, F. R. C. S., London; author of an Essay on Vaginitis, in the Medical Gazette for July, 1851:—

"I. I have not known a case of forced connexion in which rupture of the perineum has occurred. I can scarcely conceive it possible that such injury should have been inflicted under the circumstances described; for, looking to the exces-sive distention which the perineum may suffer during labour without giving way, I cannot believe that a sufficiently persis-tent and rigid erection of the penis could be maintained long enough for the commission of such injury, in spite of the re-sistance of a child of ten years of age. The medical evidence, moreover, does not appear consistent or intelligible to me. The medical witnesses depose to having found, five days after the alleged forced connexion, that the perineum was lacerated, the hymen ruptured, the genitals lacerated, the labia ulcerated, and ulceration extending *into* the rectum. This statement requires explanation on the following points:—

"If there were *laceration* of all the parts described, coexis-tent with *ulceration* of the adjacent parts, on the fifth day after the receipt of alleged violence, in what state were the lacerated edges? Were they ulcerated or not? If not themselves ulce-rated at that distance of time, what was their relation to the ulcerated surfaces? What is to be understood by 'laceration of the genitals,' as distinguished from lacerations otherwise denoted? What was the depth and character of the ulcera-tions in question? In the absence of explanation, I cannot distinguish the laceration from the ulceration.

"II. I think it physically and morally impossible that a child should have received such extensive injury by forced connexion, without having uttered such loud shrieks as *must* have roused the soundest sleepers in the same, or even in ad-jacent apartments. Had even the child been a consenting party, as it is possible from the terms on which the family seem to have lived, I do not believe that she could have sub-mitted to such violence in silence. We know full well that women in general, albeit they may be consenting parties, having every motive of delicacy or fear to insure their silence, can seldom forbear, during the first act of coition, from uttering cries, so intense is the pain they commonly suffer from simple rupture of the hymen. It is not credible, then, that a child of ten years of age could have submitted in silent endurance to mischief so incomparably more extensive and serious.

" III. No degree of laceration of the perineum, be it ever so slight, could occur without some hemorrhage; such extensive lesions as are described in this case must necessarily have been attended with a loss of blood that must have soaked the night-clothes and sheet. I have seen the hemorrhage following on very slight laceration of the perineum in childbirth so considerable as to require special surgical treatment. From the absence of this sign I infer that the perineum *was not* lacerated by sexual connexion, *forced* or *allowed*.

" IV. I do not believe it possible.

" V. Yes; I have seen a case of the kind. A girl, about thirteen or fourteen years of age, was attacked with sloughing phagedena two or three days after a single primary coitus. The disease rapidly manifested the virulent characters, extending to the thighs, nates, &c., and the girl narrowly escaped with her life.

" The post-mortem appearances in this case are perfectly in accordance with what I saw in the above; and what I have seen in others cases of sloughing phagedena.

" VI. None whatever. Such delay afforded the strongest presumption that the child was a consenting party to the act. The social condition of people living together in the manner of these persons must have rendered the child the subject of the grossest desires, and must have been most unfavourable to the development of a regard for truthfulness.

" Experience shows that a charge of this kind brought several days after the alleged crime must be received as *prima facie* evidence of its falsity.

" VII. I do not.

" VIII. I attribute the death of Mary Johnson to sloughing phagedena, following an allowed sexual intercourse with some man affected with syphilis. Such may have been the case of the prisoner, as he is stated to have had syphilis. I see no evidence whatever to bear out the opinion that the lesions in question were the result of forced connexion.

" *26th January*, 1858."

Comment on the foregoing evidence is unnecessary; as the chief point made in the first part thereof is against the possibility of connexion with the child, after the manner stated in court, without *screams* and *hemorrhage* as the consequence thereof. With respect to the question of its being an "allowed connexion" (a crime of equal guilt in the sight of the law, when committed upon a girl of this tender age), it is against the evidence and the whole tenor of the case; furthermore, if, as stated by the Judge, the perineum was ruptured, &c., it is scarcely possible to have been an "*allowed*" connexion.

My letter, with the accompanying opinions, was returned to me by Mr. Justice Wightman, with a polite note, stating that he did not propose making any further remarks beyond those already conveyed to Mr. Lawrence and myself.

With respect to the prisoner's condition, I have not been able to get any very accurate information, and, as I already stated, I was informed that the medical man who examined him had no legal qualification. About this time Mr. Lawrence wrote to me thus :—"There are very few practitioners in either of the two capitals, or out of them, possessing the knowledge of syphilis and of the diseases of female children necessary to a just appreciation of such cases as that of Amos Greenwood. There can be no doubt that the practitioners examined on the trial gave opinions altogether erroneous. *I am satisfied that this unfortunate child did not die from gonorrhœa or syphilis.* These affections are very imperfectly understood by the general run of medical men, whose evidence usually ends in exposing themselves and misleading the courts. What can be understood in the present case from the statement that the prisoner was found to be labouring under the venereal disease in an advanced stage ?"—or, let me add, as the Judge asserted, "in a very high degree."

In a letter of his Lordship to me, dated 23rd December, 1857, he says "the symptoms of the venereal disease were said to be very similar to those of leucorrhœa;" and that Mr. Jameson, the chief authority in this case, stated in his depositions, that when he examined the prisoner Greenwood, he found warts *outside* the prepuce, and several sores upon the glands; which syphilitic ulcerations were (he swore) of "*the same description as those first manifested by Mary Johnson,*" although he did not see her until the fifth day, and when, according to his own account, "there was ulceration from the mons veneris to the rectum," and all the parts in a state of "laceration" and slough. How few qualified practitioners, even though long engaged in the treatment of venereal diseases, will venture to swear to the similarity of an ulcer on a male with that exhibited on a female! Yet such an opinion must have had its weight with both Judge and Jury. And of what use would a cross-examination of Mr. Jameson, or any other practitioner giving such evidence, have been? Why, in order to make the hearers appreciate it, they should all have walked the hospitals. What had the Jury to do with scientific quibbles of this nature? The *fact* was sworn to, as to the identity of the sores ; that surely was sufficient!

Anxious to learn something of the prisoner's state, as well as to have some questions arising out of the evidence cleared up, I wrote to the medical man of the prison in which he was confined, who, in reply, informed me that " he had the remains of an indurated sore (syphilitic) at the junction of the glands with the reflected lining of the prepuce;" but that it was contrary to the prison rules to ask any questions respecting the past.

In March last I forwarded the letter which I had written to Mr. Justice Wightman to the Right Honorable Spencer Walpole, Home Secretary of State, together with a memorial, as the prayer of which I respectfully requested a further inquiry into the circumstances of the case, on the following grounds :—

" 1. That the forced connexion, producing, as stated at the trial, and upon which the Judge laid so much stress, laceration of the perineum, or septum between the anus and vagina, could not have taken place, even in allowed connexion, without the girl screaming, and attracting the attention of her master and mistress, whose bed was within *one yard* of the place where prisoner and deceased slept.

" 2. That if such violence as was asserted by the medical men took place, it would have been utterly impossible for the girl to have risen the next morning and proceeded about her ordinary work, without making some complaint, or attracting the attention of her friends.

"3. That no sign of hemorrhage was observed on the sheets the morning after the alleged connexion, nor on the child's dress at any time.

"4. That the child made no accusation against any one until she was threatened to be ' allowed to die' of the disease which had broken out upon her, if she did not confess.

" 5. That in such cases it has been well established by Sir Astley Cooper and other writers that children are not worthy of credit.

" 6. That, of the two medical men who attended the deceased shortly before her death, and made the post-mortem examination afterwards, one was an unqualified practitioner, incapable of forming a correct opinion upon such a subject; and that the other acknowledged in a letter (an extract from which was forwarded to the Judge), that he had neither read nor heard of the disease of which I and others believe the child died, although such disease has been described in books accessible to every medical man ; and that, not being acquainted with the disease or the cases referred to where similar accusations were made, he was (no matter what his other qualifications may be) an incompetent witness on that trial.

" 7. That an examination of the child by Mr. Winnard, a surgeon at Wigan, upon the fourth day after the alleged connexion, failed to discover that frightful laceration from which it is asserted the child suffered at the time, but found only the early symptoms of a malady consisting of ulceration and discharge, which I and others assert subsequently passed on into mortification, producing death.

" 8. That all the symptoms detailed at the trial are against the supposition of *rape* and *syphilis*, and accurately correspond with those known as *noma pudendi*.

"9. That the case was of an entirely medico-legal character, and that there was deficient and conflicting evidence as to its nature."

On the 13th of April, 1858, I am informed, in reply, that Mr. Secretary Walpole " can see no sufficient reason for doubting the propriety of the verdict, especially in the absence of any assertion of innocence on the part of the prisoner himself, or of his friends." Whether this wretched, illiterate, costermonger's assistant may *have* any friends, or, if he have, whether they are imbued with a belief of his innocence, and able and willing, in the absence of a cheap criminal court of appeal, or a Minister of Justice, to bring the matter under the notice of one of her Majesty's Ministers, is really more than I care to inquire about ; and as to *his* assertion of innocence, according to the prison rules, neither the Governor, the Chaplain, nor the Medical Attendant, are allowed to make any inquiries respecting a man's innocence or guilt. I therefore again appealed to Whitehall, and in respectful terms requested an order to the medical officer of the prison to make certain inquiries of the man, subject to the usual supervision. In reply, I was politely informed that no such order would be given ; and so far my efforts, not to free the convict, but to straighten what I considered to be a deviation from the course of justice, chiefly owing to mistaken medical opinion, ended.

Personally I have no interest whatever in the case ; and it is a pleasure to me to find that the Judge, in one of his last and always courteous communications, stated that he was " fully satisfied that my object in communicating with him was to assist in the furtherance of justice." A part of that endeavour was to prevent this trial at Liverpool being constituted into a precedent in medico-legal writings, as stated at page 69 of my Letter. And it was not without reason, should I have been arguing upon the right side of the question, that I conceived that intention ; for, while so endeavouring, my friend Dr. Taylor, chiefly from the information received through me, has given the case in the recently published edition of his great work on Medical Jurisprudence. At page 698 he says :—" On the fourth day she (the child) was examined by a medical man, and then she stated that the prisoner had had connexion with her." Now, Mr. Winnard, the practitioner alluded to, states the direct contrary (see his evidence, page 63) ; and while these pages are passing through the press, he has again written to me to say :—" No charge was made against any one when the girl was brought to me, and no suspicion stated either." Dr. Taylor does not say (possibly did not know) that the accusation was forced from the child by a promise and a threat. Again, he states :—" It appears from the testimony of two medical men, who examined deceased on the fourth or fifth day, that the perineum was ruptured," &c. For that statement read—when examined on the fourth day, Mr. Winnard *saw no laceration of the perineum;* but upon the fifth day Mr. Jameson, said to be a surgeon's assistant, *stated* that the perineum was ruptured. The same gentleman said it was gonorrhœa or venereal the child laboured under, and swore to the sores on the penis of the man being similar to those on the lacerated vagina of the child. Again, at page 699 we read :—" When medically examined on the fourth day, it was found that she was affected with syphilitic disease." On the contrary, when examined by Mr. Winnard, on the fourth day, he saw nothing but *vaginitis;* and Mr. Lawrence and others state, from the same data as that presented to Dr. Taylor, that she presented *no symptoms of syphilis.* It is, therefore, scarcely fair to again assert, a little farther down on the same page, that " it was also proved that she was affected with syphilis."

" That there was intercourse," says Dr. Taylor, " appears clear from the statement of the girl and the medical evidence." Let any one read the foregoing, and say that such is clear. Dr. Taylor's work is deservedly one of the highest authority in the English language, quoted and acted upon in every court of justice in the land, and it is, therefore, of the greatest importance that every statement in it, upon which either legal or medical opinions are to be founded, should be perfectly correct. Dr. Taylor does not discuss the question as to the possibility of the child having died of noma pudendi ; neither does he, in this edition of his work, describe that disease as one with which the medical jurist should be well acquainted ; nor does he quote from, nor even specify, the cases given in the Medico-Chirurgical Transactions.

From the foregoing statement may be learned the following pressing requirements :—

The necessity for professional coroners, acquainted with medical jurisprudence.

The necessity for medical registration (just now become law), by which unlicensed and posssibly uneducated practitioners are not admissible as professional witnesses.

The necessity for a Criminal Court of Appeal.

---

Since the foregoing was published in the Dublin Quarterly Journal of Medical Science, I have learned the following additional particulars of the case of Andrew Hume, convicted of murder and rape at the Nenagh Assizes of 1840, and alluded to at pages 61 and 77 of this paper, and page 697 of the last edition of Taylor's Medical Jurisprudence, 1858. There were two counts in the indictment :—First, that the injury was committed with the finger; and, secondly, that it was produced by carnal violence. The medical witness for the prosecution swore to the latter, and denied the possibility of the former. The prisoner was sentenced to be executed, but the Jury recommended him to mercy on account of his youth; and one of the most intelligent of the jurymen stated in open Court that he was not satisfied as to the act of criminal connexion. Baron Richards, the learned and humane Judge who tried the case, having also had his doubts as to the mode of perpetration of the injury, caused further inquiry to be made,—when it was found that the Crown had not produced three most material witnesses, viz., two of the three medical men who were present at the post-mortem examination, and a soldier who could have afforded most valuable evidence for the defence. The Judge's opinion was further confirmed by a very intelligent medical man who happened to be in Court during the trial. The High Sheriff immediately proceeded to Limerick for the new witnesses. The two army medical officers stated their decided opinion that the rupture of the vagina was perpetrated with the finger, and said that they had already given that opinion to the authorities! From the evidence of the prisoner's comrade, it appeared that he had been drinking deeply during the march; that upon overtaking " the sick car," the child was crying loudly, and that Hume took it to pacify it, and to relieve the mother of the burden; that the child continued to cry, but that the prisoner never left the car; that the witness, seeing the child rolled up so closely in the prisoner's great coat, remarked that he would smother it, and that a few minutes afterwards he observed blood upon the man's hand, just before he returned the child to its mother. He also stated that the prisoner was intoxicated, and some time afterwards again took the child and was out of sight for a short time; and that, when the car came up, the prisoner was by the side of the road, holding the child by the arms, with its feet upon his shoe, as if endeavouring to save it from the cold; but not, as the report says, with the child *standing* in front of him. In fact, it was this very statement of a child under eleven months old "*standing*" up on the road-side after the infliction of such an injury that first induced me to question the validity of the alleged rape. Pending the investigation, the convict sent for the medical officer of the prison, and confessed to having thrust his finger into the child's vagina while it was under his coat, as already described. Upon the recommendation of the Judge, the man's sentence was commuted to transportation.

Here I cannot refrain from adverting to the circumstance of the non-production of evidence by the Crown, where such is within the cognizance of the proper officer. At this very moment a man is undergoing sentence in a gaol in Ireland for a rape on a young child, in which case a medical witness, the first who examined her, was not produced, because, as he states to me, an official informed him that he was afraid his evidence "would damage the case." I am constrained to say that in many instances what is aimed at is, I fear, not so much the attainment of truth, as to secure a conviction.